LEGAL THRI

TRUE

JUSTICE

JOSHUA GRAYSON

Legal Thriller: True Justice

Joshua Grayson

Author's Note: This book was originally published under the name Joshua Grisham, however to avoid any confusion with another author, this book is now published under the pen name Joshua Grayson.

True Justice

Brad Williams Book 1

Legal Thriller: True Justice

Criminal attorney Brad Williams always does the right thing. Sort of.

When Brad Williams is offered a lot of money to take on a case for sly banker Jonas Baxter, he is in no position to refuse. Jonas has been charged with the attempted murder of local prostitute Tina Jade, but it quickly becomes evident that it is not the reason why the prosecution wants Jonas behind bars.

So why are they still pressing ahead with the charges?

What is Jonas guilty of?

This thrilling legal short story will take you for a ride through the courtroom and leave you with twists and turns that you didn't see coming.

CHAPTER 1

I'm glad he's dead.

It's not the right thing to think at a funeral, but it's how I feel. Benjamin James Windsor was a bastard. The worst kind too.

He cheated on his wife regularly with hookers, he never returned favors, and he never bought anyone a beer. But only the people closest to him knew how bad he really was.

His public relations team made sure that the rest of the world saw him as an out and out champion. A man of the people. A guy who would do anything for anyone.

That must have been one good PR team.

As a Senator, Benjamin achieved nothing. Nothing. But he was always there – patting the right people on the back, stroking the right egos, and singing the praises of the right people. That's how politics works. It shouldn't – but it does. That's reality. The people who rock the boat the least are the ones who find the biggest reward.

The one's who want to make a difference, the people who can change the world for the better, are laughed out of the game by the players.

Benjamin didn't laugh himself out of the game. No. He was shot out of the game.

He received a bullet to the forehead at close range. A jogger found his body one morning next to a river. He hadn't even been reported missing yet. The killer must have dumped his body in the water hoping it would take weeks to be found. Unfortunately for the murderer, a heavy downpour of rain meant that all sorts of things were washed up by the river's edge. Benjamin's driver showed up three days later, further down the river, after suffering the same fate.

But no charges have been laid.

It's not a good look for the Boston Police Department to have a murdered Senator, and his driver, and zero suspects. Not even one. I would have assumed that the department would have arrested someone by now – if only to ease the media pressure of not being able to find the killer.

Sitting in the back row of the church brings back memories of my strict Catholic childhood. I received the cane across the knuckles so many times that I still fear the smell of the cane. Whenever I catch a whiff of something similar, my heart rate rises, my palms become sweaty and face twitches. Scotch is the only thing that calms those nerves.

The church is packed with the city's movers and shakers. Politicians, judges, lawyers and criminals have squeezed in here today. Some are here to benefit their careers, and others are here to find out who actually shot Benjamin.

Even if the department went on motive alone, I'm sure they would have at least a few thousand angry locals on their list. Benjamin was a charmer, but he was also very capable at making enemies.

I am here because for the first half of my life, I considered Benjamin my closest friend. We grew up together and bonded over our joint hatred of the cane. Quite often, we would sit next to each other in detention for hours. We later attended law school together and graduated in the same class.

Benjamin quickly took the step into politics, and I spent the next twenty years defending criminals as a defense attorney. Good money – lousy job.

Early in my career, despite years of being told what to believe at a Catholic school, I was able to shake any sense of righteousness and chase the money. It meant that I stretched the rules further than they should have gone, but I never got caught.

Now, I have developed my own sense of morals. I am old enough and experienced enough to know what is right and wrong. That never happened for Benjamin. He never developed any sense of morals. Although we still had a quiet beer once a year, we had grown apart. It was always nice to say hello, but clearly, our lives took different directions.

He contacted me on the day before he was murdered and said that he needed to discuss something urgently. I was too busy to return his call – and now it looks like I will never know what trouble he got himself into.

After the casket is carried out of the stale air in the church, I gaze up to the midday sky. I am relieved to have stepped out of the church without getting accused of my many sins. Every time I step into a church, I expect a priest to appear out of the shadows and scold me for things that I didn't even know were wrong.

"Brad Williams, the defense attorney?" I feel a hand rest on my shoulder.

"I am," I turn around slowly to see a tall man, well-dressed, and in his early fifties. His eyes look shifty, and he carries with him a sense of distrust.

"I need your help," he states in a matter of fact tone.

"And you are?"

"Jonas Baxter. A close friend of Benjamin."

That means trouble.

"And why would I help you, Mr. Baxter?"

"Because there is a lot of money in it for you."

"How much?" I nod.

"What are your current fees?"

"They are-"

"Double them."

"I haven't even told you them yet, Mr. Baxter."

"I don't care. I have heard you are the defense attorney in town and I want you on my team."

I nod, standing still, contemplating the offer.

"Sounds like a lot of trouble you have yourself in, Mr. Baxter."

"That's why I need you..."

Chapter 2

Boston feels busy today.

There seem to be extra people scurrying about their daily lives, desperate to get to where they are going. I watch as a young man, typing into his mobile phone, knocks over the drink of a homeless guy sitting on the street. The young businessman scolds the homeless guy for leaving his coffee out and brushes the spilled coffee off his suit pants with aggression.

The older man, weary at existence, stares at his spilled drink as if it symbolizes his life.

Pushing through the crowd on the street to reach him, I deliberately drop my shoulder into the young man as I pass, knocking his phone onto the ground. He yells at me to watch where I am going, but I ignore his calls. One of the benefits of being 6'4, broad and strong is that once people see you, they tend to tone their voice down. The young man doesn't say much more as he bends down to pick his phone.

I throw ten dollars into the hat of the old man, and he smiles at me.

"Thanks," he mumbles.

"It isn't much," I shrug.

"Not for the money," he smiles a toothless grin. "For bumping that guy."

I laugh loudly. I would love to stay and take this guy out for breakfast, but I am too busy. We all are.

Some people thrive in the rush of a city. They love it. They love the adrenaline filled pace. Not me. Despite having to face it every day, I hate it. I would much prefer the slower life.

Jonas Baxter certainly got himself into trouble.

He has been charged with the attempted murder of a local hooker in a run-down hotel room. Jonas is married with three children, so it isn't a good look. His wife is standing by him – probably because she wouldn't know how to live life without this prick.

The charges state that he beat Miss Tina Jade five times in the skull from behind. There is no weapon, and the hooker was too drunk to remember what happened. Jonas admits to being in the hotel room with Miss Jade. He states that he left the room that night, and she was drunk when he left, however, he did not hit her.

When I arrive at my office, Jonas is already waiting for me. I nod to him and my secretary, the lovely Gillian Cooper. Leaving my office door open as I enter, I call out to welcome Jonas in.

"I didn't beat her," he states as he walks into my office with confidence.

Everyone denies their guilt. Even the ones who have been caught on camera deny their guilt until they realize there is no use fighting. Half of my job as a defense attorney is to get innocent clients off, and the other half of my job is to get the best deal for the ones that have no chance of getting off.

"There are many questions that I need to ask you before we get to that point, Jonas. Now, would you like tea or coffee?"

"No, thank you. Gillian has already offered me one."

"Good." I lean back in my chair behind my hefty oak wood desk and let the silence sit in the room. The way a man reacts under silence can tell a lot about his innocence. I watch him closely. In the silence, Jonas doesn't seem uncomfortable – in fact, he seems very comfortable with the situation. He is either very confident of his innocence, or he is overly confident in the judicial system. Either is dangerous.

"Why did you require a hotel room only twenty minutes away from your house?"

Jonas's eyes drop to the floor, "I didn't realize this was a marriage counseling session, Mr. Williams."

"It isn't. But these are questions that I need to know the answers to."

"I needed a break from my wife. She's... needy. I told her I was working out of town for the night and I booked a run down hotel where I was sure that nobody would see me. It was my chance to get away from it all."

"Then why did you invite Miss Tina Jade to meet you in your hotel room for the night?"

"Why does any married man invite a hooker to his hotel room?"

I drum my fingers on the table. "Your lying."

"And why would you say that?"

"I can see it in your eyes," I let the pause linger in the room before continuing. "Let's be straight, Jonas. You are my client. It is my duty to do what is best for you. However, to do the best thing for you, I need to know everything that happened that night. I cannot help you if you will not help me."

He stares at me, pauses and then continues, "I'll be level with you – she was my alibi."

"Why would an upholding citizen like yourself need an alibi?"

He laughs, "It was... an insurance policy."

"Against?"

"I'm a banker, Mr. Williams. And I might push the boundaries of trading sometimes. Sometimes, I make deals with people to make a lot of money, however... these deals might be viewed by some as being dishonest. I meet people at certain times and certain places to exchange information. Having an alibi means that I cannot be implicated if anything goes wrong."

"Except something did go wrong."

"Not with the meeting. Everything went right with the meeting. But with the alibi, yes."

"Could the person from this meeting be your alibi for the night?"

"No. Officially, there was no meeting."

"I understand," I don't push the point any further. "Why not use your wife as a fake alibi?"

"Because she knows where I am every part of the day. She knows the time I leave the house in the morning, how long I leave the house to go for a run, or how long it takes me to buy something from the shops. That's what happens when you live with someone your whole life. Even though she is not recording the information anywhere, she knows. But a drunk hooker, she's different. I can give them a few drinks, and then they pass out like a light. I leave for an hour and come back, and they think I've been there the whole time. The perfect alibi."

"Has it ever been tested?"

"Once. I was questioned by the Securities and Exchange Commission for information about a deal, but I denied all wrongdoing. Of course, they tracked the man I met with, but I proved I had an alibi that night. They interviewed the hooker, she said I was there all night, and the investigators didn't push it any further. Without charges, my wife never knew the difference."

I have an overwhelming urge to punch Jonas in the face.

I don't like him.

I don't like the way he uses people, or the way he has complete disregard for anyone else's feelings. I envision my fist coming off the desk and connecting solidly with his jaw. I could break his jaw with one swift punch. I've done that to men before.

But having a client with a broken jaw is not a good look in a courtroom.

Especially if his attorney has done it to him.

"So you bought her for the night, got her drunk, waited until she passed out, and left for one hour. But when you returned, she had been beaten unconscious?"

"That's correct."

"And where exactly were you during that hour?"

"Does it matter?"

"Possibly."

"I was walking the streets. Trying to clear my head," he says, clearly lying.

"And did anyone see you during that hour?"

He shakes his head.

If I were to lay a bet about this case, I would say that right now, things don't look good for Jonas.

Prosecutions like to build a picture of a person to give the jury a head start on their guilt. Right now, even I don't like Jonas. He's sleazy, under-handed, and arrogant. Jurors have been known to convict a defendant on their personality alone. It is the assumption of guilt that works against a person sometimes. We are going to have to work very hard in the courtroom to present Jonas as an upholding citizen.

This is going to be harder than I expected.

Clients that are guilty are fine to deal with, but clients who are guilty *and* evasive, they are almost impossible to defend. I need to drain more detail from Jonas if he is going to have a chance of winning.

I enjoy a challenge, and the thrill of a close case, but this is going to be harder than I expected.

"Did anyone else know that you were in the hotel room?"

"No. I never tell anyone about the hotel room. It's my own little back-up plan."

"Tell me what happened after you returned to the hotel room."

"Miss Tina Jade was lying on the bed with blood coming out of her nose. She had clearly been beaten up. I grabbed my things and left the hotel room."

"Why didn't you call the police?"

He shrugs his shoulders, "Because I didn't do it and I didn't want to get caught doing what I was doing."

"But the hooker survived and identified you, as did the hotel attendant. So the police arrested you for attempted murder. You understand that this doesn't look good."

He nods.

"Do you think that when you were out walking the streets for the hour, that someone might have sent a person to your hotel room to set you up?"

He shakes his head, "No. I wasn't followed. I've done this enough times to know how to keep my tail clean. And even if that line of questioning was true, we couldn't do anything about it. There would be no way to prove it."

"There must be video surveillance of the hotel," I state.

"There isn't. I have checked," he responds. "There are cameras, but none of them have worked in months. It wasn't exactly a secure neighborhood I was in."

The way he makes the statement with such firmness tells me he is hiding something. I glare at him, but he doesn't crack.

Slowly, I write some notes about the case, stare at the paper, and then turn back to Jonas to confirm.

"Let me get this story straight, Jonas. You told your wife that you were going to be out of town for the night and booked into a run-down hotel twenty minutes from your house. You hired a hooker for the night and gave her a few drinks. When she passed out, you left the hotel room for one hour to 'walk the streets and clear your head.' When you returned to the hotel room, the hooker had been beaten within an inch of her life. You then left the hotel, but the hooker identified you."

"That seems to be the case."

"I feel like you're hiding something from me, Jonas."

"No... I was just wandering around. I don't even remember which streets I was wandering around on."

"You were drinking?"

"No."

"I think you were. I think that you were drinking with the hooker, and wanted to go for a walk. And that is why you can't remember where you were."

"Yeah…" Jonas smiles. "Now that you mention it, I think I was drinking."

I nod and continue taking notes.

"That just leaves us with the witnesses. It was dark so I should be able to discredit what they are saying, but it depends on what the jury is going to believe. I think the witnesses might be the tipping point. The report states that the victim was drunk, and she didn't get a look at the person's face before they hit her. She assumes it was you. The police report also states that the witnesses, including the alleged victim, saw a man leaving the scene that matched your description, but they're not sure."

"Yeah, I heard it. They said they saw someone in a black hooded jumper that matches my build, but I wasn't even wearing a hood that night."

"We should be able to discredit them in court, but I will need your help with that. I'll need you to make statements around what you were wearing on the night. If we had CCTV footage of you walking around, that might help."

"There's no CCTV footage."

His statement is blunt and firm. It rouses my suspicion.

"How can you be so sure?"

"I may…" he shrugs his shoulders again, "I may have made sure that there wasn't CCTV footage."

"Why would you do that?"

He stares straight back at me, piercing me with his bloodshot eyes.

"Right, but if I needed them?" I continue.

"You wouldn't."

"Do they still exist?"

He shakes his head slowly.

I lean back in my chair, trying to consider how to move this case forward.

"That still leaves us with the witnesses. That's what the prosecution will rely on. I will see what I can think of."

"And let me see what I can do to help out."

I have a feeling that this case is going to get very heavy…

Chapter 3

The more information I find about Jonas Baxter, the more I don't like him.

I asked numerous people around town, and they all seem to have the same opinion of him – a bastard. And I haven't come across anything to dispute that opinion yet.

Apparently, the deceased Benjamin Windsor had regular meetings with Jonas. They were known to be friends around town.

That makes me uneasy.

Jonas has certainly made a good living for himself. His reputation is one of hard work and luxury – but I doubt he earned that luxury legitimately.

As I investigate his innocence, it seems that even if he is innocent in this case, he has done plenty to warrant time behind bars.

I sit at a bar near Jonas's office and find my target – a run-down middle-aged man, dressed in an expensive suit but wearing it poorly. His tie is undone, his face shows two-day old unshaven growth, and his eyes look tired.

He is a man within desperate reach of his mid-life crisis.

"Rough day?" I approach him and sit next to him in the bar.

The bar is middle of the road – not cheap, but certainly not high-end either. This is the third bar I've been in tonight, just searching for the right piece of information. And I think I might have struck it lucky.

"They're all rough days now," he moans after he looks at me.

"Banking?" I ask.

"Yeah," he swirls his drink as he looks into it. "Banking. You?"

"Not banking. I'm an attorney."

He raises his glass of scotch, "Here's to the least trusted professions in the USA."

The sarcasm in his voice hides his pain. If I were to guess, I would say his wife has left him, his boss is ten years younger than he is, and he is on the verge of falling apart.

"Been getting many wins lately?" I ask him. My tone is casual, but my question is very targeted.

"No. You have to be an insider trader to get wins these days. Those guys own the game."

"Insider trading?" I pretend I'm surprised. "That's illegal."

"Only if you get caught."

"Is it easy to trick the system?"

"Real easy if you know what you're doing. The problem is, it makes it hard for the rest of us to make any money. It ruins the whole system, you know? Those bastards break the rules, and they'll never get caught."

"Why not?"

"They're too clever. They are always one step ahead of the law."

"Like Jonas Baxter?"

He stares at me with angst, "You a cop?"

"No. I'm Jonas's defense attorney. I'm just trying to establish who he is."

"Defense attorney? Oh right, yeah, I heard that he was up for the attempted murder of a hooker. That's what happens. If you enjoy the high life too much, things get a bit wild and then – bang – it all falls apart."

"Do you know much about Jonas?"

"Yeah, he's trouble," his words are firm and direct, leaving me no doubt of their truth. "Look, I can't say much more. But I'm going to tell you something, something important. You just have to promise me one thing."

"And what is that?"

He leans towards me, and I catch a waft of his alcoholic breath, "That you didn't hear it from me."

I nod, "Sure."

"I hear that Jonas and Walter Pitt work very closely together," the man lowers his voice almost into a whisper. "You might want to start your questions there."

"And who is Walter Pitt?"

"The Presser."

"The Presser?"

"A Presser is a man that gets things done. If you want someone to convince someone else to change their minds, you bring a Presser. They 'press' people for information, if you know what I mean. Just be careful though, Walter is a dangerous man."

"How dangerous are we talking?"

"Anyone, anytime."

"If it's common knowledge, why don't the police arrest them?"

"Jonas has always had friends in high places. Benjamin Windsor, for instance, was known to be very close to Jonas. Clearly, Benjamin could pull a few strings if needed."

"Benjamin Windsor, the murdered politician?" I question. I knew that Benjamin and Jonas were friends, but I didn't know to what extent.

"That Benjamin Windsor, yes. Be careful where you tread with this case. Although Jonas has a lot of friends in high places, it is still Walter Pitt that I would be concerned about."

"And Walter and Benjamin work closely together? Are you sure?"

"A hundred percent sure. I watched it happen to a friend of a friend. He had some information that was valuable to the Exchange, and Jonas approached him for some tips. He offered a bribe, but the guy wanted nothing to do with it. So a day later, he ends up in hospital with two broken legs, and a week later, Jonas has made ten million dollars from suspect trading. Of course, the guy didn't press any charges."

"Why not?"

"Because he was scared. These guys don't stop. The only way you will ever stop guys like Jonas Baxter or Walter Pitt is to put them in the ground."

"Or keep them behind bars for life."

I ponder my own statement for a while.

This case is going to be fun...

Chapter 4

There was something in the way that Jonas avoided my question about security footage that has me concerned. Either he knows where the footage is or he destroyed it. If that information is presented to the courtroom, then I might as well lock Jonas up now. Nothing looks as guilty as destroying possible evidence.

I went to the hotel to review the security footage personally. All the cameras were broken, and any existing footage was missing. The owner of the hotel stated that he never keeps the footage unless something goes wrong. He said he didn't find out about the attempted murder charge until days later, and by that time, he had already thrown the footage out.

Of course, he was lying.

His jittery nature and avoidance of eye contact gave that away.

But across the road from the hotel, is a used-car yard. After some negotiation, I was able to view the footage from the night. At the top of end of the furthest camera, the entrance to the hotel across the street can be clearly seen.

I viewed the footage and after paying a small sum of money, I took the only copy. Used-car salesmen are the worst people to negotiate with, especially when they have what you want.

But the footage is why I'm approaching Mr. Pitt's penthouse apartment now.

I walk up to the apartment building in a nice area of town, throwing a couple of dollars at each homeless person I pass. The apartment building I enter is modern, spacious, and clearly, a person needs money to afford to live here.

When I reach the door of the top-floor room, I hear heavy footsteps approach the door. I can feel the eyes on me and then the thick door swings open.

"You the lawyer?"

I look up to the man that stands in front of me – he is over 6'6, and as wide as a hallway. In his forties, he is clearly a man that has seen a lot of action in his time. His knuckles rest on the door frame, and they are covered with the scars of past battles.

"Are you Walter Pitt?"

"I am."

"Then you and I need to chat."

The man judges me, staring at every inch of my body, and then moves the door open enough for me to enter.

The apartment I enter is huge with few furnishings, but I suppose a man the size of Walter Pitt would need a lot of room to relax.

"I'm a friend," I explain. "And I'm helping Jonas. But to help Jonas, I need you."

"Everyone needs my help, mate." There's a distinct English accent in his tone when he says 'mate.'

"English?"

"I was born there, but my parents moved out here when I was ten. I am a proud American now. Get to the point, mate. I don't have time for chitchat."

"I need you to testify that you were with Jonas the night that he was charged with attempted murder."

His whole body jumps as he laughs, "Look, mate, I like Jonas, but I am not going near any courtroom. That's just asking for trouble for a guy like me. I avoid those places like the plague. You will find that hell will freeze over before I step foot in a place like that."

"Then we have a problem."

"Jonas's problems are not my problems."

"But Mr. Pitt, it's also a problem for you."

He stares at me again. It must take a while for the information to process in his brain. He definitely qualifies as the muscle of an operation, but clearly Jonas is the brains.

"Sit down," it is more of a demand than an offer. "And tell me more."

I sit on the edge of a soft leather couch, sinking uncomfortably on the new cushions.

"If they don't pin this attempted murder charge on Jonas, they will come after you. It's what the police are saying," I lie. "They know that you are Jonas's muscle. They know that if he didn't do it, then it must have been you. If I win this case without a testimony from you saying that you were with Jonas that night, then you will be arrested within hours."

"Me? I wasn't there."

"It doesn't matter. The police want someone to go down for this, and whether that is you or Jonas, they don't care."

"But?"

"But if I get you in a courtroom, on the stand, and you testify that you were with Jonas that night, in a car outside the hotel room for an hour discussing business, then the police can't come after you."

I have Walter's attention now.

"So you're asking for me to give you money to make sure that Jonas is found guilty of attempted murder?"

I laugh out loud. I love how the criminal mind works - sell each other out at the smallest opportunity.

"No, Walter. What I'm saying is if you get up on that stand in a courtroom and testify that you were with your friend Jonas on the night of the attempted murder, then I can get you both off."

"We both walk away?"

"You do. Because you've testified that you were both together, the prosecution has no case to build against you."

"Why would you even do that? What difference does it make to you?"

"I can't imagine that you would think it was too favorable that I got Jonas off, only to throw you in the shit."

"Right... that's clever. I like the plan. What do I have to say?"

"You just have to testify that you're Jonas's alibi."

"Sounds easy," he laughs. "I'll do it."

I laugh with Walter, not for any reason, but I imagine when he laughs most people feel compelled to laugh with him.

Chapter 5

It took several attempts to lock in a time with the prosecution to talk about the free passage of information. Clearly, they think they are in front on this.

Actually, so do I.

I'm not that interested in their information, but I need the meeting to get a feel for my opponent. I want to know how they are going to play the court.

"Miss Petrie will see you now," the secretary interrupts her attack on the keyboard to relay the information.

Walking into the office with confidence, I have a pleasant surprise. Miss Anna Petrie is very good looking.

"Hello Mr. Brad Williams," she holds out her hand with a smile.

I shake it gently, "Hello Miss Petrie."

"You can call me Anna. Please sit down."

"Thank you," I try to maintain eye contact with the woman, and she stares me down. This chick is tough.

"Defending Mr. Baxter must be quite a case for you, Mr. Williams. Mr. Baxter has a lot of money to throw around, but he is also not a very nice person. How do feel about defending an asshole?"

Her comment makes me laugh - her soft, easy looks contrast the hardness in her words.

"I'm not here to make a judgment on people's characters. I'm here to defend an innocent man."

"I think innocent is a very overrated term for Mr. Baxter."

I roar with laughter. I can't believe this woman's nerve, but I like it.

"You look too innocent to be a lawyer," I smile at her.

"And you look too nice to be a defense attorney."

Our eyes connect again, and I am smitten. This woman is smooth.

"Why do you want my client so badly, Miss Petrie? It is 'Miss,' isn't it?"

She grins, "Yes, it is 'Miss.' I haven't found a man strong enough to handle me yet." She maintains eye contact, and I lose my train of thought. She is going to be dangerous in a courtroom. "But we want Mr. Baxter because he's a criminal."

"You've got nothing on this case. You don't have a reliable witness, the DNA on the body can be explained, and who've got no evidence on his whereabouts. I'm not sure why you are charging ahead with this case."

I am fishing for information. For the prosecution to push forward with this case, there must be something else that I am missing. There must be another piece of information coming.

"That is all the evidence we have at the moment."

That's the key - 'at the moment.'

Prosecutors often tell the detectives to hold off with the information so that they can present it at the last minute – hoping to catch the defense off-guard. Usually, that play doesn't have me worried, but with Jonas's lack of honesty, it does concern me this time.

"Do you have any information waiting?"

She shrugs her shoulders and smiles cheekily.

Oh, I really like her.

"Why are you after my client? You haven't even presented a plea option for him. You must want to crush this guy for some reason."

"Jonas Baxter is not a nice person. Nor does he add anything to the community. If he is guilty of the attempted murder of this woman, and I thoroughly believe he is, then he deserves to spend time behind bars. Just because this woman is not respected by members of society does not mean that people like Mr. Baxter can treat her like dirt. She needs people like me to ensure that it doesn't happen again."

"But why this soft case? If he's that bad, then why not use another case against him? A case with real hard evidence? You have nothing on this case."

She pauses, and considers her next words, "I'm surprised you don't know."

"Don't know what?"

She stares at me to see if I'm playing her, but I have lied so many times that I'm not even sure how to act honestly anymore.

"You really don't know what case I am talking about?"

I shake my head.

"Good luck with the case, Mr. Williams," she smiles as an invitation to leave her office.

I return the smile, provide her a nod, and leave with more questions than I arrived with.

This worries me.

Anything that Jonas is tied up in can be easily thrown onto me. Prosecutors quite enjoy pinning criminal activity on their opposition.

Miss Petrie seems smart enough, and sexy enough, to play me.

And the deeper I go in this case, the more I don't like it.

Chapter 6

After a full day of jury selection, the spectacle is ready to begin.

It will be interesting to see how Miss Petrie plays her case. She has enough charm to convince the jury that bacon is now a vegetable, but she is also brutal enough to destroy even the most hardened men. She will be a tough nut to play against.

There are a scheduled two days for the prosecution case and one day for me. But I won't need a full day because I'll do most of the damage during the Miss Petrie's case. I'll discredit any witnesses and destroy any evidence they try to present.

I will then present Jonas as a pleasant, compassionate man - even though he clearly isn't - and as a person who is misunderstood. The jurors will have to back my side on the basis of a lack of evidence.

My only concern is what I don't know. What does the prosecution have up their sleeve? And what is Jonas hiding from me?

"One minute," the bailiff calls out, warning that the Judge will arrive in a few moments time.

This is it.

This is my moment. A case on the big stage. My chance to shine.

I love the start of a trial.

The excitement is overwhelming.

My heart is pounding in my chest with anticipation for what is to come. The fate of the man next to me rests in my hands. It is up to me to determine how his future will play out.

I love that feeling of power.

As I stare at Jonas, I feel a sense of dominance. I can destroy this man if I want to.

"All rise."

This is it.

It's time.

The tall, broad and dominant figure of Judge Priestley enters the room. He moves slowly, with authority and composure. I like him. I like his no-nonsense attitude.

He isn't big on emotions and doesn't like it when the prosecution attempt to try a person based on anything else other than hard facts. He is my type of judge.

The courtroom seats behind me are filled by an interesting group of people. Some old folks who I see every week, some of Jonas's acquaintances, and some supporters of the defendant. But there are two faces that stand out.

It's Boston Police Department's Commissioner, Howard D. Emmons, and sitting next to him is the Superintendent in Chief, Michael O'Meara. They are both studying my client intently. This worries me.

It means I have missed something.

Something important.

I don't like that. I don't like that at all.

Chapter 7

After Judge Priestley says his piece, Miss Petrie plays her cards. She opens her statement sitting behind her desk, but when she gets into her speech, she stands and gradually moves around the table. I like the way she moves. Her hips have a gentle swing to them.

"Jonas Baxter is a man without a history of convictions. But that does not mean he is incapable of committing a crime. Everyone is innocent until proven guilty. And the evidence you will hear over the next few days will leave you no doubt of his guilt. Right now, he is deemed innocent. In three days time, your opinions will have changed."

Miss Petrie sways throughout her opening statement, and by the end of it, even I am convinced that Jonas is guilty. She is mesmerizing to watch.

She explains the evidence, reiterates that Jonas is a man without a history of convictions, and explains how this is their chance not to let him get through the cracks of our legal system again.

Interesting argument.

I watch the faces of the jury intently and pick the ones that I have to throw my defense at. Five jurors look uncomfortable when Miss Petrie begins to talk about emotions.

They are my five.

The five people that I need to target to convince them of the facts. They will not be swayed by imperfect evidence. They are the ones that will address this case on evidence alone.

There may be five sitting there, but I only need one of them.

That is a good feeling.

As Miss Petrie finishes, Jonas leans across to me and whispers, "We're still covered by client-lawyer confidentially, aren't we?"

His whisper is so quiet that no-one else could possibly hear.

I nod.

This doesn't sound good.

"I've done some bad things, Brad. I've killed and tortured people, Brad."

"What?" I look straight at him.

"I thought you should know that I'm a ruthless man before you present your first argument. I don't want you to play any silly games."

I am in shock with the words that have just been whispered into my ear.

"Mr. Williams, are you ready?" I am sure that Judge Priestley can see the confusion on my face.

I stare at my notepad while I try to gather my thoughts. Jonas's is trying to intimidate me into winning this case. Clearly, he doesn't understand how this game works.

Looking at his smug face, I want to punch him hard across the jaw. I want to break his perfectly structured nose. Arrogant prick.

"Mr. Williams, your opening statement please," Judge Priestley's voice booms me back to reality.

Jonas's statement has thrown me. It fills my thoughts as I struggle through my rehearsed statement. My opening becomes disjointed and lost.

A very poor performance indeed.

I try to dispute everything that Miss Petrie presented, but I become lost in my own thoughts. Jonas's words have thrown me off course. What game is playing?

After my dismal opening statement, lunch is called by Judge Priestley.

The second I step out of the courtroom, I grab Jonas by the arm and drag him into an empty office.

He doesn't seem fazed as I slam the door behind me with my foot.

"What was that?"

He shrugs his shoulders, "I just thought it would be beneficial if you knew what I could do if you tried to cross me."

His smile is sly, and his eyes are filled with creepiness.

"You don't understand, Jonas. You need me. If you distract me from doing my job, then you are going to jail. You treat me with respect, or the consequences for you are dire."

"No Brad," he smiles again. "The consequences for you are dire if you do not get me off this charge. I saw them there."

"Who?"

"The Police Commissioner and the Superintendent. They weren't just checking in on us."

"Then why don't you tell me why they were there, Jonas?" I step into his personal space, my face close enough to smell his foul breath.

"You don't need to know."

"This is a normal attempted murder case. That level of the Boston Police Department does not show up for these cases. They are here for another reason. What are you hiding from me, Jonas? I need to know and you need to tell me now. I can't play this game if you're not going to be honest."

"You don't need to know," Jonas says with gritted teeth. "Get me off this charge, and everyone walks away happy. If you don't get me off this charge, my friend Walter will pay your family a visit."

I slam Jonas against the wall, my arm pressed into his neck. "Don't you dare mention my family."

"Do you know Walter Pitt, Brad?"

I stare at him closely, keeping enough pressure against his neck so that he struggles to breathe. "I've heard of him."

"Let me tell you this. If I go down, Walter will not be a happy man. And you do not want to see Walter when he is unhappy. Nor does your family."

"Fuck you."

I release the pressure on his neck, and turn to walk out the door. "You mention my family again, and you will find out that prison is not a very nice place."

I walk back out the door of the small office, where a man is about to enter and use his office.

He mentions something about needing permission to use the office, but I am too angry to listen to him whine.

I am being played by Jonas and by Miss Petrie.

That makes me angry.

Chapter 8

After the lunch recess, there is a panicked air in the courtroom.

Miss Petrie looks frantic, and the Police Commissioner is talking angrily on the phone. This doesn't feel good.

"Your first witness please, prosecutor," Judge Priestley's voice booms through the courtroom.

The prosecutor fumbles through her papers, and then turns to engage in a lengthy discussion with the two men next to her.

I have a really bad feeling about this.

"May I approach the bench, Your Honor."

"You may."

I follow Miss Petrie's toned body up to the bench.

"Our first witness has... vanished."

"Vanished?"

"Yes, Your Honor."

"People do not just vanish, Miss Petrie. When was the last time you saw the witness?"

"Yesterday at 4 pm."

"Is it not possible that they may have forgotten about today?"

"No, Your Honor. The police received a call this morning that stated our witness was pulled into a white van when she stepped out of her house to go to work. At first reports, it appears that she has been kidnapped. The police are investigating, but at this time, we have no witness."

Judge Priestley stares at me.

Shit.

Chapter 9

I sit behind the desk in my office, leaning back and staring out the window when Jonas walks in.

After today's events, Judge Priestley called an early recess for the remainder of the day.

Clearly, the prosecutor was rattled, and that didn't look good to the jury.

Everyone in the room was pointing their imaginary finger at my client – which makes him automatically look guilty.

"Did you do it?" I stare at Jonas with cold hard eyes.

"I'm sorry sir, but I have no idea what you are talking about," he grins.

"I'm going to ask you slowly, Jonas. And you had better give me the correct answer. Did you organize it?"

"Now that's a better question, Brad. It's important to ask the right questions. I would have thought that lawyers would be well trained in asking the right questions."

"Where is the witness?"

"Another good question. But I am afraid I don't know the answer to that."

"Are they safe?"

He shrugs his shoulders.

"Missing witnesses will not help our case. In fact, I can guarantee that everyone in that jury box now thinks you're guilty. This is bad, Jonas."

"You said that the witnesses were a problem in this case."

"But it was a problem we could sort out. What about the other witness?" I ask, "Are they going to be safe tomorrow?"

"I don't know."

"What do you mean you don't know?"

"When you push a wheel down a hill, Brad, you have no control over how fast it will run away. Whether that witness shows up tomorrow depends on how fast that wheel is rolling."

Shit.

This is bad.

I have never felt like walking out on a client before, but that's how I feel right now.

I want to break his nose.

I want to kick him while he is on the ground.

I want to stomp on his head.

But I have one ace left up my sleeve…

Chapter 10

Returning to the court the next morning, Miss Petrie and her team present further evidence against my client.

She captures the juror's attention as she displays a timeline of events for the evening. She leaves the jury nodding their heads at the possibility that Jonas is guilty.

But my five still look like they have a touch of doubt in their eyes. They want hard evidence, not assumptions.

After she presents mostly circumstantial evidence, one of Petrie's team whispers something in her ear. The look on her face is full of worry.

This doesn't feel good.

I look to Jonas, but he avoids eyes contact with me. Damn. I could punch this guy right now. Even sitting next to me, there is a smug look on his face.

"Your next witness please, Miss Petrie. Let's hope they are ok this time."

My heart is in my mouth as the prosecutor returns to her table. I hope that fumbling of the papers is all part of the act.

The detective over her back shoulder whispers something, and then she states, "Permission to approach, Your Honor."

Shit.

This isn't good.

My eyes fall to the table in front of me.

"Granted," Judge Priestley's voice is laced with anger.

My legs are weak with nerves as I walk up to the bench with the prosecutor at my side.

"It appears that a second witness has also disappeared."

"Are you sure?" he leans forward in anger.

She nods.

Judge Priestley's fist clenches around the gavel. His bloodshot eyes portray the anger raging through his veins. Judges do not like it when the law is played with.

"Bail is reversed!" he declares in his booming voice.

Judge Priestley's hammer slams down.

"What?! That can't be done! I've paid my bail!" Jonas jumps to his feet.

"Restrain yourself," Judge Priestley demands.

"Your Honor, please understand that my client is angry and confused at your sudden decision. There is no evidence that my client has had anything to do with the disappearances, and I think it may even be unlawful to reverse his bail without any evidence."

"Do not lecture me on the law!" his voice echoes through the courtroom. "This courtroom is not a joke. A witness is protected, and I will NOT have missing witnesses on my watch! Lawfully, I can reverse the bail conditions if I feel there has been a breach of the conditions. I have two missing witnesses, and I will not have a third. Take the man into custody. Now!"

Jonas smiles, nods, and somehow, I think he knew this was coming.

As he is handcuffed, he leans across to me to whisper,

"I think you are doing are a great job, Brad. Your family would be proud of you."

Chapter 11

Again, Judge Priestley called for an early recess considering the developments of the case. But that works for me. It gives me time to get myself out of this mess.

The following morning, the prosecution's third and final witness, the alleged victim, has elected not to testify. Petrie states to the court that it is because of fear that she has decided not to take the stand. The juror's all nod.

Well played, prosecution.

As Petrie reads the victim's statement to the court, her voice is full of emotion and drama. Her hands move around perfectly, and her facial expressions display the pain the victim must have felt.

We are taken through the moments when the victim remembers entering the hotel room with Jonas, and then waking up hours later, bloodied, bruised, and beaten. She woke up to the empty hotel room and rang her pimp for help. Of course, he came rushing.

Though I am sure it was to protect his investment rather than any emotional ties to the woman.

She cannot remember anything past getting drunk — she doesn't remember the incident or whether Jonas left the hotel room.

The weight of evidence is starting to grow in the juror's box. Even my five are beginning to look convinced.

I am behind in this case. But that's fine because soon, I will make my big play. It is my chance to clear Jonas's name of the charge.

And that's exactly what I am planning to do.

I can save this case today.

I have sent my family out of town for the next two nights in case the results don't go as I expect them — however, I am confident that I can walk away from this courtroom with my head held high and my safety intact.

"Your first witness, defense," Judge Priestley sounds grumpy. "Let's hope that we can have some witnesses in this case."

"The defense calls Walter Pitt to the stand."

From the corner of my eye, I catch a glimpse of Jonas's face. The shock is clear. His mouth hangs open as Walter walks to the stand.

Walter's walk is slow, but purposeful. This is a man that is confident he can fight his way out of any situation. His oath is full of pride and strength.

"Please state your full name for the court," I stand from behind my desk and wander around in front of Walter.

"Walter James Pitt."

Walter even dressed in a suit for today's court appearance. It shouldn't matter, but something as simple as a suit can sway a juror's opinion of a witness. People naturally make a judgment on a person within the first seconds that they see them – and jurors are no different.

"And how is it that you are acquainted with Mr. Baxter?"

"Jonas and I go way back."

"Way back to where, Mr. Pitt? Can you please elaborate further?"

"Right. We first met at my grandmother's funeral. She was very active in the community, and I remember Jonas standing next to her casket with a large bunch of flowers. He had a lot of respect for her. And we have been close ever since."

"What a lovely story," I smile.

"Objection," Miss Petrie is lackluster in her objection. "This makes no difference to the case."

"Sustained. Move on, Mr. Williams."

"And how long have you known Mr. Baxter?"

"Many, many years. I'd hate to think how long ago that was, because that'll make me feel old."

That comment gets a slight laugh from the jurors. When a juror laughs it is a good thing – it means that they have trust in this man.

"And where were you on the night of the 5th of April, Mr. Pitt?"

"I was with Jonas."

"Are you sure? I remind you that you are making that statement under oath, Mr. Pitt. Do you understand that?"

"Yes, absolutely. I was with Mr. Pitt on the night of the 5th of April."

"All night?"

"No, sir. I was waiting outside his hotel room. I went to the door of the hotel room, and I saw the girl in his hotel room, and then we spent the rest of the night together. The girl was healthy when I saw her, and we never returned to the room."

"And are you certain that the girl was unharmed when you left the room with Mr. Baxter?"

"Absolutely."

"Objection!" the moment becomes too much for Miss Petrie. "This is not evidence. This is two friends looking after their own best interests. Mr. Baxter has said in his police statement that he was alone that night. This is not a reliable witness! We've already established that they're lifelong friends."

The prosecution is flabbergasted that I would pull such a stunt. It is amateur in its attempt to prove my client's innocence.

"Overruled. Continue questioning the witness, Mr. Williams. And I hope that you have some evidence to back this up."

"Thank you, Your Honor. And I assure you that this is heading somewhere." I turn back to Walter. "I would like to present new evidence to prove my client's innocence."

There is a collective gasp in the courtroom.

The Police Commissioner turns to the people beside him and discusses the new development. He doesn't look happy. Miss Petrie does not know how to react to the presentation of new evidence.

She looks nervous and worried. She had this case in the bag, and now it is about to slip away.

"I will present to the court the footage of Mr. Pitt and Mr. Baxter together on the night in question. It will clearly show that my client was not in the hotel room at the time of the attack."

"Objection, Your Honor. There was no surveillance footage available," Miss Petrie argues her case. "We have established that earlier in the case. The cameras at the motel were quite simply not working."

"Overruled. Mr. Williams, please explain what is happening here."

"Certainly, Your Honor. Yes, it is true that the surveillance footage was not working in the hotel that night. Nor were any cameras on the street. However, there are a number of cameras across the road at the car yard that clearly shows the entrance to the hotel. I would like to present this as evidence to the court."

"Go ahead," Judge Priestley nods.

The bailiff rolls the television into the front of the courtroom. "Please, bailiff, play the video."

The bailiff does as instructed, organizing the footage to play.

"Whilst we cannot see the hotel room, we can see my client and Mr. Pitt exiting the hotel entrance at exactly 10.43pm that night."

"Objection. This does not disprove the attempted murder charge; it merely shows that they were together."

"Overruled. Let's keep the tape rolling."

The footage plays, and we watch as Jonas and Walter are clearly shown looking at the camera together and then walking out of the hotel entrance and into a sleek SUV waiting on the street. Both men enter the car.

"As you can see, both my client and Mr. Pitt are together here on the night of the 5th of April. And if we continue to watch the footage, we will see the defendant's pimp enter the building… right here."

I point to the screen, and we watch as a tall, scruffy man enters the hotel building.

"And from the footage we can see the number plate of the SUV my client entered," I point to it on the screen, making sure everyone's attention is focused on the car.

Suddenly, two white flashes brighten in the SUV.

Clearly, they are gunshots.

And now I wait.

I watch as the confusion on the prosecutor's face turns from anxiety into panic.

"That number plate… on the 5th of April?"

"Yes. The date is on the video. Just down here in the bottom corner of the video. I know that it is confusing for you, but this clearly shows my client's-"

"Wait!"

"Miss Petrie, you had better have a good reason to interrupt the defense," Judge Priestley is unimpressed.

"I do," she scurries her papers, and the Police Commissioner behind her stands. "That is the number plate of the official car for Benjamin Windsor! That is his car... on the night he was murdered!"

The courtroom erupts in a commotion.

The penny drops.

The noise and movement is overbearing.

"Your Honor!" Miss Petrie shouts over the noise, "The prosecution moves to withdraw the case against Jonas Baxter."

"Are you sure, Miss Petrie?"

The commotion in the courtroom is now loud.

"Yes, Your Honor."

"Then let the man go."

The gavel slams.

The case is won.

Jonas is let go by the court guards.

My client is innocent of the attempted murder of Miss Tina Jade. Completely innocent of the charge. Her pimp is now her main suspect.

However, both Jonas Baxter and Walter Pitt were together on that night.

Together as they murdered my old friend, Benjamin Windsor, and his driver, after they entered his SUV.

Clearly, it was a business deal gone wrong.

That is what Benjamin was trying to tell me about the day before he was murdered.

Jonas quickly races towards the exit of the courtroom, hoping to escape amongst the commotion. But as soon as his feet step out of the courtroom, he is arrested by five quick-moving uniform police officers.

The men in blue.

Some of society's finest people.

He is slammed to the ground, struggling to get free.

But there will be no freedom for him. Ever.

A murdered politician means life in prison for the cold-blooded killer.

Walter Pitt bumps my shoulder as he looks for another exit, but there is no escaping this. The handcuffs are quickly thrown onto his wrists.

Those two men will never see freedom again.

As their presence disappears, the smile on my face emerges.

"Did you know the evidence would drop them in it?" Miss Petrie asks over my shoulder, as I leave in the commotion.

I smile.

"When I saw the Police Commissioner here, I knew you were looking for something else. You never thought he was guilty, did you?"

"Not of the attempted murder," she shakes her head. "But we didn't think you would prove it in court."

"Now, go and chase that pimp for beating up that girl. Put him behind bars."

"Yes, sir," she smiles sweetly.

"Until next time, Miss Petrie..."

<u>End</u>

Legal Thriller:

True Justice

Joshua Grayson

Also by Joshua Grayson:

Killer Justice

Protecting Justice

Real Justice

Look for more coming from Joshua Grayson soon!

If you enjoyed this short story, please leave a review.

21491653R00046

Printed in Great Britain
by Amazon